I WANT TO BE A CHRISTMAS TREE

The story of a little tree with a big dream

By Lori Lynch

Dedicated to my son James.
May you always believe in yourself, follow your dreams,
and know that anything is possible.

Brooklyn Writers Press
Brooklyn, NY
www.brooklynwriterspress.com

978-1-952991-16-5 Hardback ISBN
978-1-734572-48-3 - E-Book ISBN

LCCN 2020921483

I Want to Be a Christmas Tree

The Story of a Little Tree
with a Big Dream

By Lori Lynch

It was a beautiful sunny day on Abelia Lane as Nick and his Nanna returned home from the nursery excited to plant their new tree! The other trees in the yard looked on as they unloaded the truck.

"I wonder what kind of tree will join us this time," said Sal the oak. "Another just like me would be great," said Benny the American beech. "I think one of you is plenty," said Lindsey the lemon tree as she frowned at Benny.

Natalie the northern cedar chuckled. "Look here, you two. That little tree is not like any of us. I believe... yes... it's an evergreen!"

"An evergreen?" laughed Benny. "We'll see how long he lasts!"

James the evergreen was so excited to be in his new home, a place to grow big and strong and one day fulfill his dream of becoming a Christmas tree to a loving family. As he looked up at the other trees, he quickly realized how much bigger and stronger they were. He also realized he was the only evergreen. *I will not be afraid,* he told himself as he got up the courage to say hello to the other trees. *I am brave!*

"Hello, my name is James." One by one the trees turned away from him, rustling their leaves. *I don't understand*, he thought, "*Why won't they talk to me?*"

"Listen," said Benny. "You're just an evergreen. "You will never grow to be big and strong like us and we don't want to be friends with a little tree."

"I will grow up big and strong like you," said James. "And when I turn seven, I will be picked to be the Christmas tree for Nick and his family and bring them happiness!"

The other trees laughed at James. "That's a silly dream," said Benny.

James did not let the other trees make him feel sad, but as the days and weeks passed, he continued to feel more alone.

One night, as James was falling asleep, a small voice woke him.

"Psst. Are you awake?" James looked around but couldn't figure out where the voice was coming from.
"Down here! Hi, my name is Dominic, the baby fern."
"Hi, I'm James! You surprised me!"

"I heard what the other trees said to you. Don't let them make you feel sad. I want you to meet Caroline the squirrel and Scotty the cardinal, they're my friends and they'll be your friends too."

James was excited to have three new friends and also
because his favorite holiday season was finally starting.

"I just love this time of year!" he said. "You see that Christmas tree
in the window? That's my dream. I want to be a Christmas tree and
bring happiness to a loving family. Once I turn seven, I will be ready."

"That sounds nice, but what if you don't get picked
to be a Christmas tree?" asked Caroline.

"I know I will be a Christmas tree," he said proudly.
"I believe if you have a dream in your heart and the
courage to follow it, anything is possible."

Christmas time came around again like it always did, and it wasn't long before James saw Nick and his Nanna heading out to the yard, just as they did every year.

Is it time? Please pick me, he thought, as he stood tall and proud. He was now seven and ready to be a Christmas tree! But Nick and Nanna walked right past James with just a quick glance.

Later that night James saw a truck pull up to the house with a Christmas tree tied to the top. "Is that a Christmas tree? He wondered. It can't be. Why didn't they pick me?"

"Don't worry. Maybe they're just waiting until next year to pick you," said his friends. "I hope you're right," said James. "They better pick me soon, otherwise I'll be too big to fit in the house!"

James tried to stay positive, but each year that passed brought more disappointment. Just as he had told Benny years before, James had grown big and strong and now towered high above the other trees in the yard.

"My dream is over," he thought. "Now I'll never be a Christmas tree."

"Never let go of your dream," said Dominic. "Just keep it close to your heart and have the courage to keep believing in it, just like you always told us."

James was thankful for Dominic's kind words. Even though he knew he would never give up on his dream, he felt so sad inside and to make matters worse; it began to rain.

The rain continued to fall, and it wasn't long before a tired Scotty flew into the yard, landing on James' branch.

"There's a huge storm coming!" he shouted.

"Scotty, round up all of our friends and tell them they can take cover in my branches," said James.

"What if I blow away?" said Dominic.
"Just hold on tight and don't let go," said James as he stretched out his branch. "I will make sure you're safe."

James was afraid, but he knew he had to stay strong and brave for his friends.

James had never seen such a storm!

After it finally passed, James quickly looked around
for his friends. "Is everyone okay?" he asked.
"Yes, we're okay," they said.
"You saved us, James, you saved all of us!"

James was so thankful his friends were safe, but it didn't take him
long to realize he was the only tree left standing in the yard.

As Nick and Nanna returned home, they couldn't believe what they saw. All of their beautiful trees were gone...all but one.

I wish there was something I could do, thought James as he noticed them walking towards him.
He stood tall for them, even though he just wanted to rest his branches.

"You sure have a powerful spirit," said Nanna as she patted James on his trunk.

A few months later, James noticed a large
truck pull into the driveway.

"Oh no! I think they are taking me down!"

"Where are they taking you?" yelled Caroline.
"I don't know! I don't know," he said.

No sooner could he get the words out of his mouth
when he heard "Timber!" and fell to the ground.

"We're coming with you!" shouted his friends, and
just like that Dominic, Scotty and Caroline jumped
into his branches as the truck drove away.

James had no idea where they were taking him.
A few hours later, the truck stopped and he was lifted out.

When James opened his eyes, he saw skyscrapers all around him.

He stood there puzzled and then heard a familiar voice
come over the microphone. "Nanna?!" he cried.

"What is she doing here?"

He listened closely as she told the story of the terrible
storm that destroyed their home and how one tree from
her backyard, the only survivor of the storm, had become
a symbol of hope and strength for her family.

"This tree will now represent peace and hope for the world
and bring happiness to people everywhere," she said.

"I give you...

THIS YEAR'S ROCKEFELLER CENTER CHRISTMAS TREE!"

With those nine words, a sea of electricity ran through James and he lit up in a million different colors.

"AHHHHHHHHHH!" James yelled out.
"You're a Christmas tree!" his friends shouted.

"I'm a Christmas tree? I'm a Christmas tree? I'm a Christmas tree!" "My dream came true!" he said.

James stood tall and proud. As Dominic, Caroline and Scotty looked on they remembered the words their special friend had always said to them...

"If you have a dream in your heart and the courage to follow it, anything is possible."

ABOUT THE AUTHOR

Lori Lynch, born in Wilmington, DE, found her passion early in life. At four years old, she began a lifelong journey to become a dancer, a dream that took her to New York City, where she has lived since 2002.

Besides performing, Lori has devoted her career to teaching and mentoring children for nearly two decades. Working with children every day and helping them develop self-confidence is a gift she treasures.

I Want To Be A Christmas Tree, The Story of A Little Tree with A Big Dream is a book ten years in the making. Publishing the book is another dream come true for Lori. She hopes it can serve as a reminder to children that anything is possible and that they should never give up on their dreams.

Thank You for Reading
I Want to be a Christmas Tree
The Story of a Little Tree with a Big Dream

If you enjoyed this book, please consider leaving a short review
on Goodreads or your website of choice.

Reviews help both readers and writers. They are an easy way to support
good work and help to encourage the continued release of quality content.

Connect with Lori Lynch
authorlorilynch@gmail.com
O @lmlwrites

Want the latest from the Brooklyn Writers Press?
Browse our complete catalog
brooklynwriterspress.com